MW01165264

St. Mary Grade School
602 E. 8th Street
Dell Rapids, SD 57022

Montana

by Patricia K. Kummer,
the Capstone Press Geography Department

Content Consultant:
Harry W. Fritz
Department of History
University of Montana

C A P S T O N E   P R E S S
M A N K A T O ,   M I N N E S O T A

C A P S T O N E   P R E S S
818 North Willow Street • Mankato, MN 56001
http://www.capstone-press.com

Printed in the United States of America.

Library of Congress Cataloging-in-Publication Data
Kummer, Patricia K.
    Montana/by Patricia K. Kummer (Capstone Press Geography
    Department).
    p. cm.--(One nation)
    Includes bibliographical references and index.
    ISBN 1-56065-528-3
    1. Montana--Juvenile literature. I. Capstone Press. Geography Dept.
II. Title. III. Series.
F73103.K86 1998
978.6--dc21

                                        97-9496
                                           CIP
                                            AC

Photo credits
Capstone Press, 4 (left)
G. Alan Nelson, 10, 22
Cheryl Richter, 8
Root Resources/Larry Schaefer, 16
Lynn M. Stone, cover
Travel Montana/G. Winderwald, 4 (right); S. Shimek, 5 (left);
    D. Broussard, 5 (right); Mike Sample, 6; Donnie Sexton,
    12, 18, 25, 34
Unicorn Stock/Aneal Vohra, 20; Larry Stanley, 29; Royce
    Bair, 30
Brian Vikander, 26, 33

Table of Contents

Fast Facts about Montana

State flag

Location: A
    Rocky Mountain
    state in the
    northwestern
    United States
Size: 147,046
    square miles
    (382,320 square
    kilometers)

Population: 870,281
    (1995 United States
    Census Bureau figures)
Capital: Helena
**Date admitted to the
    Union**: November 8,
    1889; the 41st state

Western meadowlark

Largest cities: Billings, Great Falls, Missoula, Butte, Helena, Bozeman, Kalispell, Anaconda, Havre, Miles City
Nicknames: Big Sky Country, Treasure State

Bitterroot

State animal: Grizzly bear
State bird: Western meadowlark
State flower: Bitterroot
State tree: Ponderosa pine
State song: "Montana" by Charles E. Cohen and Joseph E. Howard

Ponderosa pine

Chapter 1
Glacier National Park

Montana is sometimes called the Treasure State. This is because copper, gold, and silver lie under the ground of the Rocky Mountains. People also say one of Montana's greatest treasures is Glacier National Park. The park is in northwestern Montana.

The U.S. Congress created Glacier National Park in 1910. Its name came from glaciers that formed the land long ago. A glacier is a huge sheet of slowly moving ice. Glacier National Park covers 1,538 square miles (3,999 square kilometers) of Montana.

Each year, about 2 million people visit Glacier National Park. Most of them drive along

People say Glacier National Park is a Montana treasure.

Glacier National Park has five different habitats. It is unusual for one area to have so many habitats.

Going-to-the-Sun Road. It goes over the top of the Rocky Mountains. The park also has 700 miles (1,120 kilometers) of trails.

Habitats

Glacier National Park has five different habitats. A habitat is the place and natural conditions in which a plant or animal lives. It is unusual for one area to have so many habitats.

The first habitat is grassland. It has very dry land. Many grasses grow there. This kind of land is usually found in the middle parts of continents.

The second habitat is hardwood forest. It has plenty of moisture. The temperature can be warm or cold. Trees grow well there. This kind of land is usually found on the East Coast of the United States.

The third habitat is evergreen forest. It has cold temperatures. Only a few kinds of trees grow there. This kind of land is usually found in Canada and Northern Russia.

The fourth habitat is alpine tundra. It is too cold for trees. Some plants grow there. This habitat is usually found in Alaska.

The fifth habitat is polar. It is very cold. Temperatures are nearly always below freezing. It is hard for plants and animals to live there. This habitat is usually found only in very high mountains.

The Last Best Place

Montanans love their state. They sometimes call it the Last Best Place. Each year, more tourists come to Montana. Some of them decide to make it their home. They think Montana is the Last Best Place, too.

Chapter 2

The Land

Montana is in the northwestern United States. It is the fourth largest state in the nation.

Montana is the largest Rocky Mountain state. Idaho is to the west. Wyoming lies to the south. They are Rocky Mountain states, too. North Dakota and South Dakota are Montana's eastern neighbors. The country of Canada lies north of Montana.

The Great Plains

The Great Plains cover eastern Montana. These high, rolling plains gave Montana the nickname of Big Sky Country. The wide-open space makes the sky look big.

Montana is often called Big Sky Country.

Small mountains rise across the central plains. They include the Bearpaw Mountains and Little Snowy Mountains.

The Great Plains have Montana's best farmland. Cattle graze on its grasses.

The Rocky Mountains
The Rocky Mountains stand in western Montana. Montana's Rockies have more than 50 ranges. They include the Bitterroot, Absaroka, and Beartooth.

Montana's highest point is Granite Peak. This is in the Beartooth Range. It is 12,799 feet (3,840 meters) above sea level.

The state's lowest point is also in the Rockies. It is on the Kootenai River. This is 1,800 feet (540 meters) above sea level.

The Continental Divide
The Continental Divide twists through Montana's Rockies. The Continental Divide is a region of high ground that divides the river system. Rivers west of the Continental Divide run into the Pacific Ocean. Rivers east of the Continental Divide flow toward the Gulf of Mexico.

Montana's highest point is in the Beartooth Range.

The Clark Fork, Columbia, and Kootenai rivers are west of the Divide. The Missouri and Yellowstone rivers are east of the Divide. The Missouri river begins in Montana near Three Forks. It is the nation's second longest river.

The St. Mary and Waterton rivers flow north. They empty into Hudson Bay. Montana is the only state that has rivers which flow east, west, and north.

Wildlife

Grizzlies and black bears live in Montana's forested mountains. So do mountain goats and bighorn sheep. Prairie dogs build towns on the plains. Rattlesnakes also live there.

Bald eagles, hawks, and grouse live in Montana. Trout and grayling swim in its lakes and rivers.

Climate

Land east of the Continental Divide has hot summers and cold winters. Land west of the Divide has warmer winters and cooler summers.

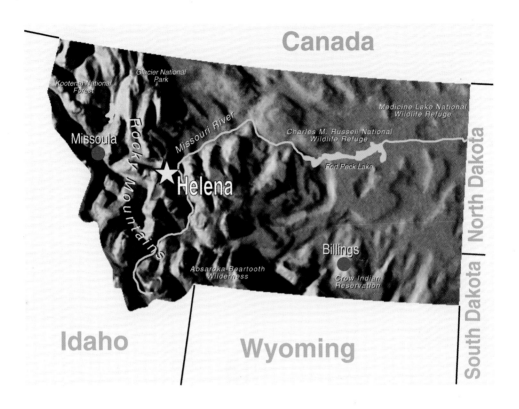

The Rockies receive more rain and snow than the Great Plains. In some years, the mountains receive 25 feet (seven and one-half meters) of snow. The plains receive up to 15 inches (38 centimeters) of rain and snow.

Chapter 3
The People

Because many people have moved to Montana, the state's population has grown in recent years. Montana's wide-open spaces draw many newcomers. Some movie stars have bought ranches. Missoula attracts artists and writers.

Some newcomers still have jobs in their old states. They work from their homes in Montana. They use computers to connect to distant businesses.

Retired people have moved to Montana also. Missoula and Bozeman rank among the best retirement cities. Hamilton and Kalispell have many retirees, too.

Montana's wide-open spaces draw many people.

The Crow are a major Native-American group in Montana.

An Uncrowded State

Montana ranks 44th among the states in population. It ranks fourth in land area. That means Montana is not very crowded. There are about five Montanans per square mile (13 per square kilometer). Only Alaska and Wyoming have fewer people per square mile.

About 52 percent of Montanans live in or near cities. Most of Montana's large cities are in the Rocky Mountains. Billings has the largest population on the Great Plains. About 48 percent of Montanans live in rural areas.

Montana's Largest Population Group

Almost 93 percent of Montanans are white. Early white settlers moved to Montana from all parts of the United States. Most were miners and farmers. Some people from these family groups still live in Montana today.

In the 1880s, European immigrants arrived. Miners came from Ireland, Wales, England, Italy, and Poland. Farmers arrived from Germany and Norway. Lumberjacks came from Sweden.

Native Americans

Native Americans make up 6 percent of Montana's population. This is the nation's fourth largest percentage of Native Americans.

About 50,000 Native Americans live in the state. Blackfeet, Crow, Sioux, Assiniboine, and Cheyenne are some major groups.

Most of Montana's Native Americans live on reservations. A reservation is land set aside for use by Native Americans. There are seven reservations in Montana. Native Americans farm on the Blackfeet Reservation. They make electronic goods at the Fort Peck Reservation. The Flathead Reservation has a large resort.

Asian Americans

About 4,000 Asian Americans live in Montana. Chinese people first arrived in the 1860s. They ran laundries and restaurants in mining towns.

Japanese Americans arrived during World War II (1939-1945). They were moved from the West Coast. The U.S. government thought Japanese Americans might take Japan's side in the war. The government forced many Japanese Americans to work on Montana's sugar beet farms.

Today, Southeast Asians are Montana's largest Asian-American group. Many own farms in the Yellowstone and Bitterroot valleys.

Other Ethnic Groups

About 2,000 African Americans live in Montana. Fewer African Americans live in Montana than any other U.S. state. Montana's first African Americans arrived in the 1860s. They worked as miners and cowboys.

About 12,000 Hispanic Americans live in Montana. Most of their families came from Mexico. Many of them are farm workers.

Some of Montana's African Americans work as cowboys.

Chapter 4
Montana History

People first lived in Montana at least 12,000 years ago. Some tools used by these early people have been found near Helena.

By the 1700s, Native Americans lived in Montana. The Salish and Kootenai came from the Pacific Northwest. They settled in the Rocky Mountains. Blackfeet, Crow, and Cheyenne moved from the east. They lived on Montana's Great Plains.

U.S. Explorers and Fur Traders
In 1803, the United States purchased land from France. This included most of Montana. Soon, U.S. explorers crossed this new land.

Lewis and Clark National Forest may have been one of the places the two explorers passed through.

Meriwether Lewis and William Clark entered Montana in 1805. They explored the Missouri, Blackfoot, and Yellowstone rivers. Lewis and Clark wrote about Montana's many buffalo and beavers.

In 1807, trader Manuel Lisa set up Montana's first fur-trading post. It was located at the place where the Bighorn and Yellowstone rivers meet. U.S. trappers caught many beavers. They sold them at the fur-trading post. Beaver pelts were the most valuable furs.

Gold Mines and Cattle Ranches

In the 1860s, prospectors found gold in Montana's southern Rockies. A prospector is a person who looks for minerals such as gold or silver. Thousands of prospectors rushed to the area. Mining towns sprang up. Helena was one of them.

During these same years, cattle ranching came to Montana. Ranchers brought longhorn cattle from Texas. The cattle grazed on the grasses of the Great Plains. Ranchers sold beef to the mining towns.

A monument marks the battlefield of Little Bighorn.

Indian Wars

In 1851, the U.S. government set aside reservations for Native Americans. Gold miners and cattle drivers crossed those lands. Native Americans attacked these invaders.

In 1876, U.S. Army troops arrived. General George Custer attacked Native Americans at the Little Bighorn River. The Sioux and Cheyenne killed Custer and all his men. The Native

Americans won the Battle of the Little Bighorn.
But they were soon forced back onto reservations.

Copper Mines and Railroads

People called the town of Butte the Richest Hill on
Earth. Miners found rich veins of copper there in
the 1880s.

Marcus Daly and William Andrews Clark owned
Butte's largest copper mines. They became rival
copper kings. Daly founded the Anaconda Copper
Mining Company.

Railroads opened in Montana in the 1880s. They
shipped copper and cattle across the nation.

The 41st State

In 1889, Montana entered the Union. It became the
41st state. About 143,000 people lived in Montana.
Helena became the state capital in 1894.

The railroads brought more settlers to the new
state. Some settlers built wheat farms in the
northeast. Others started sheep and cattle ranches in
the south.

Food processing plants opened in eastern towns.
Mills made flour from wheat. Other plants packed
meats.

**In the 1880s, people called the town of Butte the Richest
Hill on Earth.**

World Wars and Depression

In 1917, the United States entered World War I (1914-1918). Montana farmers sent wheat and beef to feed the troops.

During the war, drought hit the state. There was little rain. Crops died. Then the Great Depression (1929-1939) hit the nation. Prices for crops and cattle fell. Mines closed.

The U.S. government started the New Deal. This program provided jobs for thousands who were without work. More than 10,000 workers built Montana's Fort Peck Dam.

In 1941, the United States entered World War II. Montana's farms and mines helped the war effort.

Postwar Growth and Problems

After the war, mining and lumbering increased. Oil wells gushed in northeastern Montana. A large aluminum plant opened in the west. Coal mining grew in the southeast. Lumbering increased in the northwest.

Heavy mining and lumbering hurt Montana's environment. In the 1970s, state leaders passed laws to protect its land and water.

After World War II, lumbering increased in the northwestern part of Montana.

During the 1980s, hard times hit Montana again. Prices for oil and coal dropped. Lumbering was cut back. The Anaconda Company closed its copper mines. Drought ruined crops.

In the 1990s, Montanans started some new programs. They tried to bring new businesses to the state. They also looked for new ways to use Montana's treasures.

Chapter 5

Montana Business

About 80 percent of Montana's workers have jobs in service industries. Mining, forestry, and farming are also important to the state.

More people work in farming than in manufacturing. Montana is one of the few states where this is true.

Mining and Forestry

Coal and oil are Montana's leading mineral products. The largest coal mines are in the southeast. Montana's largest oil field is the Williston Basin on the North Dakota border.

People still mine gold, silver, and copper in the Rocky Mountains. Sapphires are mined near Philipsburg.

Coal mining is an important business in Montana.

Logging takes place in Montana's forests. Douglas fir is the leading tree for logging.

Agriculture

Wheat is Montana's largest crop. Spring wheat grows in northeastern Montana. Winter wheat grows in southern Montana.

Barley, hay, sugar beets, and potatoes are other important crops. Sweet cherries grow in northwestern Montana.

Montana has some of the nation's largest cattle ranches. Sheep ranches and hog farms are found throughout the state.

Manufacturing

Lumber and plywood are Montana's leading manufactured goods. Meat packing and dairy goods rank second. Aluminum and oil products are other important manufactured goods.

Service Industries

Real estate is a leading service industry. People make a lot of money selling land and homes in Montana.

Montana has some of the nation's largest cattle ranches.

Thousands of people work in the tourism industry. They serve several million visitors each year. Visitors to Montana spend about $1 billion each year. Hotels, restaurants, and ski resorts make a large share of this money.

More than 74,000 Montanans are government workers. Some of them provide services in Montana's state parks. Others work at Glacier National Park or the national forests.

Chapter 6

Seeing the Sights

Montanans and visitors enjoy the state's wide-open spaces. Many hike in its forests. Some ski down the mountains. Others boat and fish on Montana's rivers. Its cities are also interesting places to visit.

Southwestern Montana

Southwestern Montana is known as mining country. Helena started as a mining town. The state capitol building stands there today. It is made of Montana granite and sandstone. A copper dome tops the building.

Butte is southwest of Helena. Visitors there learn about Montana's copper mining. They can

The state capitol building stands in Helena.

see the Berkeley Pit. This is an open-pit copper mine. The World Museum of Mining has an 1890s mining camp. William Andrews Clark's Copper King Mansion is in Butte, too.

Bannack is south of Butte. This was once a gold-mining town. Today, it is a ghost town. People left Bannack in the 1930s. Its buildings still stand.

South Central Montana

Bozeman is the largest city in south central Montana. The Museum of the Rockies is there. Visitors can see exhibits on the dinosaurs that once lived in Montana.

Absaroka-Beartooth Wilderness is southeast of Bozeman. Montana's highest mountain peaks are there. Hikers can travel more than 700 miles (1,120 kilometers) of mountain trails.

Yellowstone National Park is south of the wilderness. The original entrance to the park is in Gardiner, Montana. But most of it is in Wyoming.

Southeastern Montana

Billings is Montana's largest city. It is a trading center for Montana's coal, oil, and cattle. In the summer, Billings hosts a rodeo each night.

The Crow Indian Reservation is southeast of Billings. Little Bighorn Battlefield National Monument is on the reservation. Visitors can see where Native Americans defeated Custer's troops.

Makoshika State Park is far northeast of the reservation. Visitors can see tyrannosaurus and triceratops fossils there.

Northeastern Montana

Scobey is in the northeastern corner of Montana. It is in the heart of Montana's wheat-growing land. Pioneer Town is nearby. Visitors learn about life in an early farm town from its 40 buildings.

Medicine Lake National Wildlife Refuge is southeast of Scobey. White pelicans and Canada geese nest there.

Charles M. Russell National Wildlife Refuge is southwest of Medicine Lake. Mule deer, pronghorns, and elk live there.

North Central Montana

Boaters enjoy the Upper Missouri National Wild and Scenic River. They can follow Lewis and Clark's route. Since 1805, little has changed along this part of the river.

Great Falls is southwest of the Wild and Scenic part of the river. This is Montana's second largest city. It was named for the falls on the Missouri river. The C.M. Russell Museum Complex is in Great Falls. C.M. Russell was a Montana artist. His art is displayed there.

Ulm Pishkun State Park is just west of town. Pishkuns are high cliffs. Early Native Americans killed buffalo by driving them over pishkuns.

Northwestern Montana

Mountains, national forests, and wilderness areas cover northwestern Montana. The state's third largest city is there, too. This is Missoula.

The Smokejumper Training Center is headquartered in Missoula. Firefighters learn how to become smoke jumpers. They parachute from airplanes to put out forest fires.

The National Bison Range is north of Missoula. A small herd of buffalo grazes there.

Libby is in far northwestern Montana. This is a logging town. South of town, treasure seekers pan for gold. Skiers head north to Turner Mountain Ski Area.

Kalispell is east of Libby. This town is in the middle of the Flathead Valley. Visitors enjoy rafting, fishing, and hiking. From Kalispell, many people drive east. They head for Glacier National Park.

Montana Time Line

10,000 B.C.—People are living in Montana.

A.D. 1700s—Flathead, Blackfeet, and Cheyenne people are living in Montana.

1743—Francois and Louis Joseph de La Vérendrye see Montana's Big Horn Mountains.

1776—The United States declares its independence from England.

1803—The United States buys most of Montana as part of the Louisiana Purchase.

1805-1806—Meriwether Lewis and William Clark explore Montana for the United States.

1807—Manuel Lisa builds Montana's first fur-trading post.

1846—The United States gains the rest of Montana when England gives up land south of the 49th parallel.

1862—Gold is discovered at Grasshopper Creek.

1876—General George Custer and his troops are killed by the Sioux and Northern Cheyenne at the Battle of the Little Bighorn.

1877—Chief Joseph surrenders near the Bearpaw Mountains, ending the Nez Percé wars.

1881—Marcus Daly opens a copper mine in Butte.

1889—Montana becomes the 41st state.

1895—The University of Montana opens in Missoula.

1910—U.S. Congress establishes Glacier National Park.

1914—Women win the right to vote in Montana.

1917—Jeannette Rankin of Montana becomes the first woman elected to the U.S. House of Representatives; she votes against the United States' entering World War I.

1934-1940—Fort Peck Dam is built.

1951—An oil boom begins in eastern Montana.

1973—An updated state constitution goes into effect.

1983—The Anaconda Mining Company closes its mining operation in Butte.

1985—The Science and Technology Alliance is formed to find new ways to use Montana's natural resources; the alliance ends in 1997.

1996—Theodore J. Kaczynski is arrested in a cabin near Lincoln on suspicion of being the Unabomber; the Freemen, a group that opposes the government, surrendered to the FBI after an 81-day standoff on a farm near Jordan.

Famous Montanans

Dolly Smith Cusker Akers (1901-1986) First woman and first Native American elected to Montana's state legislature; born on Fort Peck Indian Reservation.

Gary Cooper (1901-1961) Actor who won Academy Awards in *Sergeant York* (1941) and *High Noon* (1952); born in Helena.

Marcus Daly (1841-1900) Founder of the Anaconda Copper Mining Company in Butte and the nearby city of Anaconda.

John Horner (1946-) Paleontologist who discovered nests of dinosaur eggs (1978) at Egg Mountain near Choteau; born in Shelby.

Chet Huntley (1911-1974) Television newsperson (1956-1970); retired in Montana and organized a skiing area at Big Sky; born in Cardwell.

Dorothy M. Johnson (1905-1984) Montana State University graduate and novelist; the movie *The Man Who Shot Liberty Valance* is based on her writings; honorary member of the Blackfeet tribe.

Mike Mansfield (1903-) Miner who served Montana in the U.S. House of Representatives

(1943-1953) and Senate (1953-1977); served as the U.S. ambassador to Japan (1977-1989).

Dave McNally (1942-) Baltimore Oriole who became the first and only pitcher to hit a grand slam home run in a World Series (1970); born in Billings.

Janine Pease-Pretty on Top (1949-) Educator and preserver of Native-American culture; president of Little Big Horn College on the Crow Indian Reservation; won a MacArthur grant in 1994 to continue her study of Native-American life.

Plenty Coups (1848?-1932) Crow chief who worked with the U.S. government to help the Crow keep some of their Montana land; born near Billings.

Jeannette Rankin (1880-1973) First woman to serve in the U.S. House of Representatives (1917-1919 and 1941-1943); worked for Montana women's right to vote; born in Missoula.

Charles M. Russell (1865-1926) Cowboy and artist famous for paintings of Montana's cowboys, Native Americans, and scenery.

James Welch (1940-) Novelist and poet whose works are based on the Blackfeet and Gros Ventre; grew up on the Blackfeet and Fort Belknap reservations; born in Browning.

Words to Know

Continental Divide—a region of high ground that divides the river system; rivers to the west flow into the Pacific Ocean, and rivers to the east flow toward the Gulf of Mexico

drought—a period of little or no rainfall

glacier—a huge sheet of slowly moving ice

habitat—the place and natural conditions in which a plant or an animal lives

prospector—a person who looks for minerals such as gold or silver

reservation—land set aside for use by Native Americans

rodeo—a contest in which cowboys and cowgirls ride bucking broncos and rope cattle

spring wheat—wheat that is planted in the spring and harvested in late summer; its grain is white

winter wheat—wheat that is planted in the fall and harvested in the spring; its grain is red

To Learn More

Fradin, Judith Bloom and Dennis B. Fradin. *Montana*. From Sea to Shining Sea. Chicago: Children's Press, 1992.

LaDoux, Rita. *Montana*. Hello USA. Minneapolis: Lerner Publications, 1992.

Markert, Jenny. *Glacier National Park*. Chicago: Child's World, Inc., 1993.

Steele, Philip. *Little Bighorn: Great Battles and Sieges*. New York: New Discovery Books, 1992.

Winter, Jeannette. *Cowboy Charlie: The Story of Charles Russell*. Orlando, Fla.: Harcourt Brace, 1995.

Useful Addresses

Charles M. Russell National Wildlife Refuge
U.S. Fish and Wildlife Service
P.O. Box 110
Lewiston, MT 59457

Copper King Mansion
219 West Granite Street
Butte, MT 59701

Fort Belknap Indian Reservation
P.O. Box 249
Harlem, MT 59526

Glacier National Park
Park Headquarters
West Glacier, MT 59936

Little Bighorn Battlefield National Monument
P.O. Box 39
Crow Agency, MT 59022

Montana Historical Society
P.O. Box 201201
Helena, MT 59620

Museum of the Rockies
Montana State University
South 7th Avenue and Kagy Boulevard
Bozeman, MT 59715

Internet Sites

City.Net Montana
http://www.city.net/countries/united_states/
  montana

Travel.org—Montana
http://travel.org/montana.html

Montana Online
http://www.mt.gov

Glacier National Park
http://www.nps.gov/glac

Index